Further Outside the Box

Five Fables for Expanding into the Quantum Field

Volumes 1-5

John-Randall "J.R." Hofheins

Foreword by Gary Kociskewsi

Inclusions by Chaz Randall, Swaranjoti Kaur and others

September 2017

Also published as:

New Frequency Fables:

Inducing ourselves a more expansive life of founded satisfaction

For my Students,

By my Students

Expander and The Little Box:

Thinking much further outside the box

Part of the "New Frequency Fables" Series

By John Randall "J.R." Hofheins

Copyright 2018

Foreword

Like most college students, my perception of the world didn't end up where it started off, and thinking I had it all figured out is pretty much an understatement. My name is Gary Kociszewski. I graduated from Troy University with a B.S in psychology and a minor in the field of ABA. I will be attending classes at the University of kings College London in the coming semesters pursuing a degree in neuroscience. I can go on to bore you with more academic credentials but that would not help facilitate the energy I am conveying to you. You see, energy and flow is everything and everything is energy and flow. This concept is the embodiment of Professor Hofheins' ideas and teachings. I met J.R. Hofheins my senior year in college when I was a bit more refined. You know, full time student, employee, parent, husband, everything had a time and I had a regimen that made the military look easy. I was and still am a science guy. I mean you name it and I studied it. I love it; it makes me happy, and at that time I would have told you I knew the path to peak brain performance, I was wrong. It wasn't until the end of my senior semester when I enrolled in Hofheins class that I would realize our minds were capable of much more than we could ever of fathomed.

Chances are, if you are taking one of Hofheins classes, then you study a science. If you study science, one of the most important questions you ask yourself is why? Hofheins provides a compelling and clairvoyant perception into not only the mind but also the human thought process and flow of energy, including the "whys." The sensation and perception of our external environment is synonymous with our biological and internal environments, which is understood and clearly conveyed by Hofheins to all his students. His book, Further Outside the Box, is an extension of those ideas and facilitates the flow of energy and frequency to the higher self- while also illuminating that we are a product of our thought process. The book is a guide to the expansion of self and the understanding of universal oneness. As a student, a mix all the other pressures of life, we forget that we must think greater than our environment. This is the lesson I learned from Hofheins teachings the semester I was lucky enough to stumble upon his class. I was having a discussion with my student advisor and the issue of having to take one more psych class to satisfy credit hours arose. Hofheins class was packed full of neuroscience concepts so I happily obliged and enrolled. What I learned that semester not only altered my perception of the universe, it changed me as a person. Neurons had formed new synaptic connections and the plasticity of my brain was taking new shape. My understanding of energy had been conceived and the germination of new thoughts was beginning to bare fruit. These are the important concepts embodied in this book.

Continuing on in the field of neuroscience brings about many new and exciting opportunities for experimenting and the gaining of knowledge for myself. This little fables book and the concepts it contains bring to me a newfound appreciation for not only science but for the up coming experiments I will have in life. I take with me from this book the understanding of the energy and frequency of all things. I am grateful for the chance to have experienced Hofheins sagacity, which has helped guide my perception from where it was to where it is and pointed out the fact that no one has it all figured out, not even neuroscientists, and that's ok.

Gary Kociszewski

B.S Psychology/ ABA

One day a large segment of the population- all of whom, each of whom are more like the Wind and flow like Water- silently agreed to think similarly about lots of things in life. While they were each and all collectively, Infinite and flexible, they unknowingly agreed to box their windiness and to contain their water's flow.

Even while being eternal, with total expansive capacity to the point of infinity, they pared down their abilities, dialed down their perspectives of themselves as Eternal Life Energies and got into "The Little Box" together.

Why? you might ask, if they were infinite free and flexible beings who could live freely and lightly in joy upon the earth, doing whatever felt like "life" for them in the moment, would they curtail that kind of experience to live in a box?

Security- They felt more secure when they played to be "finite" beings. There seemed to be too much spaciousness; they did not know what to do with such vast freedom and joy, living in love. So they chose to create some delimiting beliefs into their own internal thoughts and practiced them into being. Focusing on how secure it was to have only a few beliefs... to also have other people who were more comfortable being expansive and free to tell them what was "right" and "wrong" and to generally give them direction from outside themselves...they had some warm sense of security within.

Then little by little a few "boxed" humans began to feel somewhat antsy, like there had to be more to be experienced and they looked around inside the box where all they found was too few things for a "Wind blowing freely" and "Water flowing fluidly" kind of being to be able to enjoy living.

So what some of them did was to jump outside the box, just on the other side of the thin cardboard wall, to see what else there was to experience. There! There were some more things to experience outside the box that were better and more numerous than what was just on the inside of that box right next to where they were standing. Yes, they were breathing a bit more; experiencing a bit more. They were OUTSIDE the Box!

When they looked around the exterior of the perimeter of the box, they found that there were a few more things, that were of more plentiful, colorful, enjoyable variety than what was inside the box. The more they walked very closely to the outside walls of the box, remembering what was inside the box, they were experiencing a bit more newness, a bit more numerous ideas, experiences, people and opportunities than what was inside the box.

Then, after a while, the perimeter around the outside of the box got old as well. There needed to be something new again, More new stuff. "But I am already outside the box, what else is there to do? Where else is there to go for more exploration? It's a bit scary to look out there any further away from the box. Maybe I need to try getting back inside the little box to see if there is anything new to do inside there".

So some of the humans who had gotten out of the box to explore it's closest perimeters, went back inside the box to check out what was going on. "Whoa!" One human said. "How stale the air is back in this box. But it's feeling warm and secure.... however it's sickening how old and musty this place is. I think I'm going to puke". Then, that human and a few others climbed back over the box walls to the closest outside perimeter again.

"Now that we are out here again, now even THIS feels old and musty! What are we going to try next?"

One person standing out just a few steps further from the box was faced away from the little outside group, looking out into the expanse. What was there? "Nothing. Nothing but Air".

That one "Expander" human started taking very, very slow steps toward the empty expanse. Silently she kept stepping forward. Feeling the discomfort of the total unfamiliar feeling of the vastness of what seemed like Infinity. Some little something within her was in harmony with whatever was "out there".

With every step, Expander felt a bit more free of the "containment" in which she had sequestered herself to in the box, then around the exterior of the box. Now she was vaguely recalling that there were a few humans out there who were in some way "comfortable" out there in the expanse. They were the humans to whom Expander and the other boxed humans had looked to for what to think and believe and how to act and....Those were the humans who were already recognizing that they/we/ all humans really belong to the Expansive Infinity.

Expander, walking forward, still slowly and with a tiny increase in momentum, keep focused forward.., willing to be willing. She was willing to see what seemingly few other humans were already seeing with their non-physical eyes and hearing with their infinite ears (which she was unaware she and everyone else has, until now).

"Creators", That word came to Expander's imagination. "Creators" what does that mean?", she thought. The word so resonated within Expander it began to feel like it was filling up her body with some sort of energy. "Well, I, I, I FEEL so in harmony with that word. I feel like a creator myself", she thought almost out loud, as she moved a little faster.

The farther she went into the open air of the unending expansiveness, the more she felt the spaciousness, the freedom, that she at one time felt and shed most of, back when she knew she was that which was more like "Wind" and which "fluidly flowed like Water". Now, she was feeling like who she really was meant to me. It was almost a "solid" feeling, but solid didn't quite fit the feeling....."Substance; I feel like a living animated Substance of Value".

Expander knew, after walking so far into the seeming nothingness that she was not really going anywhere in particular. She was just out, experiencing the expansiveness..."The Wind, the Air, the Infinite Energy that is so in harmony with who I really feel like is me. I really feel alive. Even though I don't now know where I am; I know that I can be the real me". I feel like...no...I know, I have everything I need because I am beginning to see and feel like who and what I Am".

After sort of feeling around in the feeling of that expansive Infinite atmosphere, Expander began feeling more "at home" in the openness, where things were not so defined and confined. "This feels unfamiliar and while I am tempted to feel scared, I somehow can get in touch with that harmonious feeling inside me that tells me that I am the substance of Life and Wellbeing. I am a creator". It was then that she "turned another corner".

Expander became more fully aware of who she is as sort of, sort of...well, the molder of her life. Acknowledging that she is a creator prompted her to feel like doing something. She felt good enough and comfortable enough in this environment that she began to sense a warmth within, that was also detectable around her. Closing her eyes for a minute or three to feel this warm, wellbeing feeling that was primarily within her, she enjoyed it there as well as around her. Standing still, it felt like a "whoosh of fresh breath and an internal shower all at the same time". Energy rose within her body. Clarity of thought and emotion sort of "happened", as she was standing there.

Now, this was beginning to feel like "home" of sorts, to the happy one. "This feels good", Expander said. "I can be my wind-like spontaneous self, my water-like, flowing self, which can allow the Wisdom in the expanse that is filling me all the time, to give me insight on what I want to do then inspiration on how to do it. I just have to pay attention to it".

Creator; Expander began realizing that the warmth she was sensing within was also surrounding her, was the Life Energy that is there for every human. The answers to the questions, the "solutions to the problems" was all in the Energy, in the Expansive Infinity that seems like nothingness and nowhere. In fact, it is full of Life; Life of which Expander was a part. She is an expression of the Infinite Life Energy, as is every human, even those who forgot who they were; who went to hang out in and around The Little Box (ugh, the thought of that brought up nausea that made Expander know she wanted to think about something different).

As Expander stood there, feeling like herself, other humans who were also wandering, exploring and learning about who they really were, began to show up as well. As they began to talk together about what they had discovered so far, they realized that they could, together, begin thinking about similar things that would be fun, even helpful to others. They could think of clarifying ideas to help humans who were also sensing a degree of readiness to try an experience "outside the box".

They individually began to realize that whatever they thought, along with clear emotion, began to swell up inside themselves and became something that felt good to them. As they continued to attend to that good feeling, swelling "thing" inside them, they soon were able to experience that in life. They could each look throughout their lives and realize how they had played a role in formulating their lives along the way. Not that they would have chosen a second time everything that happened, had they known how all of this works, but it did show their ability and capabilities. They are each creators.

Realizing that as creators, Expander and her newly forming community, could begin to create a group, a neighborhood, maybe a new City,....in which everyone realized that they/we humans are Infinite Life Energy in a body on the earth and that we each are capable of internally making energy changes in ourselves, that then begin molding the energy around us into the shape we have been shaping within ourselves.

They soon learned that what they were doing by focusing on what they Do want, they were allowing the biological brain neurons of the old thought patterns/ways of living to disconnect as the brain neurons also began to reconnect in the new different ways to make what they wanted.

It was clear to Expander and her new similarly-minded friends, that the first step in experiencing this new model for living and loving and assisting others in a totally different way....they had to not only get out of the old confining box, they had to walk from the box into the unfamiliar unknown, which appeared to be nothingness but is where everything that is Life and Love actually thrives.

Expander And The Little Box was conceived one afternoon as I was sitting quietly and allowing incoming ideas on how to convey to my online undergrad students, the idea that humans are infinite and limitlessness. Over the years students continue to refer to what we are doing in the courses as "thinking outside the box"; they really needed to see that actual life is way beyond that tired cliché.

Energy has been moving so quickly in the world, around the earth, in the universe that many, many ideas, entities, ways of doing things, perceptions of how things work, are obsolete and archival. The little phrase at hand, "thinking outside the box" is one such idea. That phrase is really an indication of still holding onto what we formerly believed to be security, only a bit less-so than being inside this contrived box of human conversation and thought.

The box is just as "made up" as everything else in our physical realm. Congruent with the Laws of Creation...

We Exist- always have, always will in some form

All is one, One is All

What we emit out, comes back in like-kind

Change is the constant

When we agree that there exists a "box" out of which we can think we first confine ourselves on a slight lesser degree. Then also, we begin to touch another bit of awareness unveiling around this matter of being infinite limitlessness. It's like we are starting to open our eyes just a little to say, "HEY! We're all in a box. That girl over there, got out and did something nobody in the box agreed with; they warned her not to do it. She climbed the wall, did it anyway and found she loved doing it. It didn't work out the first time, but she enjoyed it and kept shaping it. Now she has something over which everyone marvels". Then she moves on to the new next.

The box did not exist; we somehow tacitly and collectively created the box; but not all of us. It appears to me that we created the box in order to mis-dimenuate everything into something we thought we could control, for some sense of security, to feel autonomous over a tiny, tiny "kingdom" ....in the corner of a box.

In actuality, the beingness of Infinite Limitlessness is always trying to burst out of us. Many of us deny it outlets for various artificial limiting ideas that seem "reasonable".

The idea of being reasonable was the first idea that began to wake me re: confinement as I lead staff in undergrad contexts, as I counseled students, staff and clients, as I taught undergrad students year after year. I was tired of hearing adults telling students to be realistic, to be reasonable. This is where my former life, my "Christian" experience comes in.

Having spent about 10 years meditating on the bible passages that talk about humans being one with God, God being spirit/formless air; and again being filled with all the fullness of God" and again "faith is substance....what was made and seen was made of that which is not visible" and "greater works than these will you do" and "all of us with unveiled faces, gazing at god's glory are being transformed into the same image as we gaze at God's glory, are transformed glory to glory to glory, by Spirit". I knew humans are spirit like God is, and can do even more than what God does. Why? Jesus said it John 14 (we let it say what it says). We are Spirit, along with god. Infinite Limitlessness. It is all the same energy, just like the same sap in the tree trunk is also in the tree-branch, just like the wave is one with the ocean.

You may call this Life-Force Pranic energy "god" or "God", Universe, Chi or whatever. Or you may choose to just know this Life-Giving Energy is there and that it is clarity, understanding, Unconditional Love, Insight. It is the C## frequency 432hz of everything that lives on earth. It is totally resonant with who and what you and I are, because it **is** what we are. You do not change its essence by using different names.

I no longer identify myself as "Christian" nor do I identify as "being" a part of any other religion (yes Christianity is a religion, read the bible to find out), group, sect, or the like. I will say that after over 44 years of daily focused meditating on the bible, reading the bible through many times; after studying the bible, getting two degrees in bible; After teaching the bible in churches as well as in colleges; after training pastors to work effectively with people...after all of that- and I am glad I went through that 44 years- it led me further onward (through Christianity) into real joy, happiness, calm spiritedness, into what the Psalmist called a "wide place. While I am no longer a church bitch (bitch=dependent upon, subservient to), I do still find the Life Source Energy naturally bringing to mind many beautiful, helpful, generally clarifying bible passages which I have at close recall from the meditating-decades, that are making more sense now.

I live with a knowingness far enough into the vast expanse of Nothingness, the Air ("our Father in the Air....") that I Know that which people refer to as god. It is living pneuma, expanse; God is Spirit, the bible says, Pranic Life-Force Energy/Chi; It is everything, including me, including you. We are one spirit with Spirt. I Know ever expanding clarity which continually produces calmness in my core which then emanates out to the rest of me then out to others as well. What is helpful to me is that my earth based mind, does not know HOW to do anything, it is my Pranic Energy level mind (of which I am an expression) that knows how to do things, knows the true understanding of everything. Could this be why the bible says in Colossians 3:1-ff to stop looking at the ground and set your mind on things above earth plane? See things are connecting for me at rapid-fire speed.

Yes everything is Energy. It is being demonstrated repeatedly by quantum physicists, by neuro scientists, science writers and other science based practiioners. Spiritual teachers have been saying it for years. It is all through the bible. By the way, you cannot read the black words on the white page and understand anything of the bible. I was taught that at age 10; I veered away from it while around "studious" folk who were well meaning; had to return to feeling the vibration beneath the words in order to soak the life from the parts where it existed. One example, is that Jesus was teaching about his body being the "bread" that they all needed to "eat" and his blood the wine that they all needed to "drink", IF they were going to be connected with him. Many, even some of the closest ones to him, walked away. He didn't care. There is only unconditional love for everyone. Unconditional love allows you and I to choose to see things the way we want to see them. However, Jesus' response to those walking away and to the rest who were hanging with him was to say, "My words are Spirit and are Life". I saw what that meant one night while on a 36 hour silent/solitude retreat years ago. It was connecting with what I began experiencing as a young pre-teen, which is, you feel the energy of clarity emanating, suffusing your pores, your spirit, your organs when something resonates with your core energetic being. Experience is way prior to logic. Logic based in energy-based experience works clearly and effectively.

Living spontaneously, like wind blowing seemingly haphazardly, but always with the purpose of pure joy (again, the bible plainly states numerous places that Joy is the reason for living and is the energy for thriving), is aligned with living Freely and lightly, with living this "spacious free life" on the planet.

It was not my purpose to turn to bible teaching. The bible was part of the basis used for catapulting me forward beyond christianity into actual freedom of living in love and joy on the earth. Now, I simply follow the core spirit impulses for delight and enjoyment as the Wind that I am. The bible has many places that are helpful in re-orienting me back to core reality of "Everything is Energy", much like an inspired poetry book has, like R.W.Emerson has written, like Rumi, like others, like myself, like YOU.....when we are clearly allowing the flow of Life Energy to have freedom in and around our earth experience.

Thanks for reading Expander and The Little Box. Carry on into the expanse, ever expanding into more of your true natural self.

John-Randall "J.R." Hofheins November 2017

New Frequency Fables v 1-5

Expander and the Little Box- Living Much Further Outside the Box v1

Expander and the MORE v2

Expander and the Energy Cloud v3

Expanders New Nexts, v4

Expander Uncovers NOW v5

Expander and the MORE

From the New Frequency Fables series, v2

By John Randall "J.R." Hofheins, 2017

Sort of an Introduction

I think I am feeling the same thing that Expander is feeling- The MORE; which is out where Nothing IS. Where the empty Nothing is, MORE is sort of hidden. My interior guidance tells me when I am "hot" and when I am "cold". ...I'm "hot", btw, along with Expander. So we keep moving on into the wonderful Nothing so that Something can show up and be discovered as MORE than I or anyone else ever thought possible while looking out there, from an earlier frequency.

Expander had gotten tired of being in the box. It felt so limited and confining. After feeling the bit of freedom of more options outside of the box, when she and others climbed over the wall to experience more, she eventually discerned that there was more, and that MORE was drawing her to it.

She had been gazing out into the MORE, toward where Expander felt like the MORE might be, when she rather naturally began moving toward that so subtle magnetic pull. That MORE "out-there" where there seemed to be nothing, was where there was something. It fact there was something more, she could just sense that it was so.

She had tried every other option she could detect was there, but Expander felt sort of "bad" inside when she tried to stay where she had been. She knew that a "bad" feeling inside was not what she wanted to keep feeling, so she kept moving, sensing from within, sort of like playing "hot and cold" game. That's the hide and seek game Expander assumed everyone played at one time or another, where one hides or hides some object then another person comes out to try and find the object while the ones who know, say "hot or cold" depending upon how close or far away the seeker of the object is to the hidden object.

So, for Expander, the something more, turned out to be something much MORE. It seems the expansive sense of nothing, the empty feeling is deceptively where everything else IS.

Expander had moved into the expansive nothingness and began to feel the warmth of LIFE within her own self, her own body. She then began to have pleasant feelings, then pleasant experiences of meeting others who were also drawn to the MORE.

As the others and Expander wondered about what to do out here as they wandered about in the Nothing place-since every time they moved forward a little bit- they felt a new empty feeling, which was kind of becoming familiar now. The inner feeling was disconcerting for a moment each time it happened but then they remembered that things would soon catch up with their movement and they would feel full again, usually in another new-ish way.

Gradually, Expander and company began feeling that the practiced process and the corresponding feeling experience was simply their normal. They were beginning to think like this, to sort of expect that this is how living actually works.

How living actually works. "Hmmmm", Expander stopped and relaxed a moment to see what further ideas might come from what she and others had discovered so far. That was a part of "how living works", was to feel desire for something more; allow oneself to be okay with that something-unseen to come closer/or take the inspired steps toward it; lean into the nothingness feeling expectantly; then it leads right back into one's ever expanding Self within. It becomes homey-like again, and each time. Nothingness, which feels empty-like, leads right back to something MORE which is always located back inside Oneself.

The Expansive Oneness of the Energy World is what Expander discovered she is made of. She liked to softly imagine the Energy of LIFE to be like a huge Cloud which is Life-Energy for everything. Everything is alive in its own way because the huge Cloud is so huge (bigger than anyone knows or can imagine) that it can afford to use little pieces of itself to extend into each plant, into each fish, into each stone, each human, each ….into each everything. Everything is alive in its own unique way from the common natural Source of LIFE, the Infinite, eternal Energy Cloud.

Still stopped in her "idea getting" state, Expander was able to feel into the picture of the Energy Cloud seeming like it was separate, but sticking pieces of its cloud energy into each being and entity on earth and probably elsewhere as well, making everything sort of the same thing inside.

Everything being the same on the inside led Expander into a possible way to understand the idea even further. It reminded her of a few examples in nature. The wave of the ocean is called a "wave" but is really still quite simply the ocean in a different shape right "there". "Hmmm" again, as she was allowing that to sink in. Then a question: "What is the difference between a Tree and the Branch of the Tree? Whenever we refer to a 'tree' we refer to the whole thing as 'tree'. The thing we call a 'tree' has lots of named parts, like roots, trunk, bark, limbs, leaves, blossoms, sap, and more"... she wonderingly sat.

Maybe the idea of the huge Energy Cloud animating everything on earth by projecting pieces of its energy-cloud-ness into each entity on earth and in the air can be sort of understood by the wave and the tree branches. Ocean forms the wave of its own self. Tree extends the branches from itself and flows the same sap into them. That's a picture of oneness in snapshots of the earth.

Energy-infused Expander felt more expanded than ever after experiencing the Life flow of leaning into the Cloud-like Life-Energy for more clarity. She felt familiar with the expansive Cloud Energy now. "It is a place I want to keep returning to because there I feel so much substance within myself. I experience so much life and pure enjoyment just being associated with it" she sort-of- thought in something like non-words.

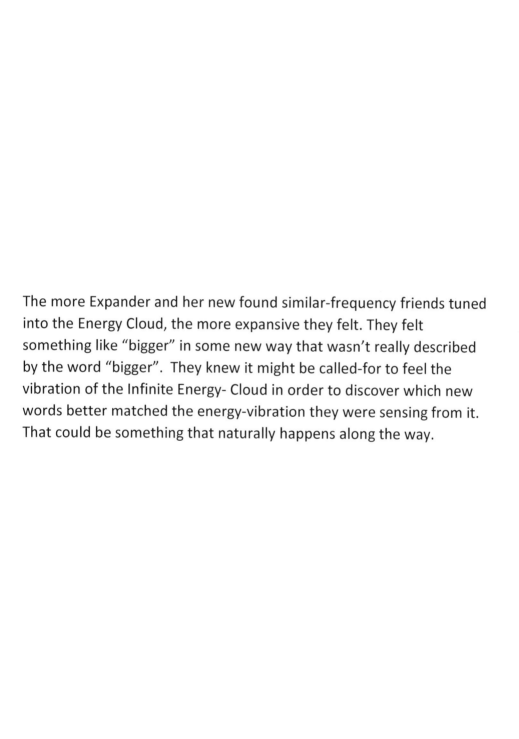

The more Expander and her new found similar-frequency friends tuned into the Energy Cloud, the more expansive they felt. They felt something like "bigger" in some new way that wasn't really described by the word "bigger". They knew it might be called-for to feel the vibration of the Infinite Energy- Cloud in order to discover which new words better matched the energy-vibration they were sensing from it. That could be something that naturally happens along the way.

Then, the more they tuned into the All-One Energy-Cloud of which they knew they were permanent part, the more they knew they could use what they were feeling for shaping the energy- which they actually are- into something new, something next, something wanted. At one time it seemed that they were shaping the energy outside of them in the world; now they were understanding more precisely that they are really shaping the energy within themselves. Expander and her friends did this by following the feeling states within themselves to change themselves a bit for the purpose of having new experiences on the earth. They were learning!

Expander said "it seems that now we are coming to know that we as part of the Energy Cloud, are shaping our energy to forms aligned with what we want to experience next; we, as Energy beings, are therefore frequencies; we shape our own energy differently, into a further enjoyable feeling-state then shift to new frequency states. We can do that in a bigger frequency shift or smaller ones. Since we change frequency states, there are new experiences, new people, new things, new joys on those new-to-us frequency registers. So we are really not changing the world around us. When we think we are changing the world, we are actually changing ourselves; that then shifts US to a different frequency scenario".

Shifting the energy within one's body so as to experience a different frequency, rather than doing things to "change the world" externally was a very new idea to Expander. "That's A little far-fetched from what I thought I knew", she said to her friends. I will continue to lean in to the Energy Cloud to see what illumination can be swirled around this idea" for me. So she did.

Expander was easily getting accustomed to tuning into the Energy Cloud. It was feeling really natural to her, since it is from there that her life extends. Things are just easy and clear there. It is so easy to simply bring the sense of what she received from the Cloud's silent vibration messages, to each earth experience she has. She noticed that she is learning by experience; learning by something like "absorption". She realized that the process of gathering information was easy and natural because, she is the Cloud much like the wave is the ocean. The Cloud is her, much like the ocean is the wave. Expander said, "It really is more accurate to say that the feeling of being separate from the cloud is the oddity, not the other way around".

"Apparently, lots and lots of humans on earth (not the animals and such but the people) have forgotten who they are and where we are from", Expander conjectured to herself. "We actually ARE the Cloud of Energy that covers and inhabits and energizes everything on the planet; the Cloud IS us."

"Leaning into the Energy Cloud, which is infinite and eternal, you discover that you exist eternally as infinity as well. You are the same thing" Expander heard inside, with her non-physical ears. As she mentally came back to the physical realm from tuning into the Cloud again, she felt more clear. She really loves it there at the Cloud. Expander lives in anticipation of orienting and re-orienting herself to that vibrant Energy of Love which is so freely unconditioned. She feels like she will be able to naturally carry that "tuned in" state with her as she explores the physical realm she has formed for herself so far.

True to her name, this is how Expander learned to continue expanding. Since that is the nature of energy, which is always in motion, that is what happens even when she isn't paying attention. The movement of energy is much like the wind's blowing wherever it wants to blow. No one knows where it came from and no one knows where it is going; that's exactly what we are. And so we go, and blow, and flow like the eternal Wind, the Infinite Energy Cloud, which Expander and we freely, really are, in love and joy...More and MORE, expanding ever more, we Are....

Last Page

Things out there can maybe only be slightly felt or detected from "here", with one's internal, non-physical ears.... non-physical eyes. The only thing "here" or "there" anyway, is different energy frequencies- nothing is solid. It's kind of like a caterpillar's antennae-feelers sensing its way along in life. Back there, (or back here, depending on where you are) things seem dim, slight but extant.

Feeling for a next-frequency feeling-state or being-state from the one we are currently in, cannot tell us what that next experience is going to be like. There are only whiffs of it in the air upon occasion and only as we desire it or sort of reach for it. It takes a relaxed knowing that the All One is All Love-unconditioned LOVE. If we lean into, peer into, restfully absorb into the Energy "Cloud" of the Universal One Energy, we find an increasingly immense sense of Wellbeing. Being in True Home... at one with the One from which we come forth, we know a Knowingness, that has expansive perspective, which then allows all things to come into order for us. The natural by-product of this experience is an inner calm composure. This calm composure, eventually -after practicing relaxed absorbing into that from which we came forth-can be known in many/most/all scenarios that we encounter in this earthly arena.

Knowing ourselves as a piece of the all-Love Energy Cloud, leaning in to soak up more of a sense of our own essence from the Cloud, the idea of being separate from that Cloud dissipates. As the sense of Oneness overtakes our relationship with the Cloud of Life Energy, it is easier to recognize ourselves as flexibly free like a river flowing, spontaneous like the Wind blowing; Lovingly knowing ourselves as The ever expanding MORE.

The New Frequency Fables Writer

J.R. Hofheins writes little books, teaches undergrad students in subjects of psychology and moves around a bit simply because it feels naturally exciting to do so. All of this for the sake of enjoying and facilitating more clarity about life, love and the exploration adventure on the earth. He more than lives in the mountains of North Carolina. (I wrote this, I wonder why I/ we tend to write little bios in third person? Trying to give the appearance that we had someone else write it for us?, Hmmm)

2017

Expander and the Energy Cloud

The New Frequency Fables series, v3

John-Randall "J.R." Hofheins

2017

An Introduction

Exploring energy-based living and loving has been going on for me since I can remember. It was not clear what this non-physical confluence was when I first encountered The Energy Cloud. It was much further along my path that it became clear to me what it was I was sensing, getting, leaning into. I was around 6 years on this planet at the earliest acknowledgement point. Realizing itself to me more fully as I could receive its revelations, It was allowing me to change my life along the way. I'm not sure where I would be or if I would "be" "here" had this reality not been shown to me in what felt like a scenario of almost dire need.

Later around age 10 there began to be encounters where, during meditating on bible passages, the experience of The Energy Cloud clarifying my life experiences and religious teachings was unmistakably life-giving. The Christian environments did not get it, accept it nor fit with it for the most part. I tried to go with it for decades using what was shown to me from the bible *by the Cloud*, much like song lyrics or poem verses are used, to give me transcendent understanding above the conflicted, debatable thought in every physical environment I entered, especially beyond the material based, limited explanations of the church and scholars regarding the bible. They were always incapable of getting the fuller Spirit/Energy clarification that was meant.

There have been various attempts to contextualize this energy experience for myself, using religion, philosophies, metaphysical groups, and the like. Some lines of thought are more helpful than others. In any scenario, I know it works. It is LIFE. Quantum Physics and recent neuro scientists are repeatedly demonstrating the energy-based reality and moldability.

Consider this approximation at prompting people to consider who we humans are and of what we are capable, as just that- an approximation. It is getting at what is going on for our sensation of actual LIFE and Thriving.

Thanks for engaging this Series. Happy unveiling of who you actually are and of what you are capable.

It isn't really accurate for me to think of the Life Energy as a "Cloud", thought Expander. However, as I am living in the world of third dimension, it is helpful to do so. Using physical representations to convey non-physical reality breaks down the meaning at some point, but does help me to that point.

Expander had been leaning into, feeling the essence of the Life-Force Energy on and off and on and off, enjoying every second she could get closer to it. In the process of leaning in, an image came up for her. This was the cloud image-not that she excavated, but which came into her imagination- which was such a helpful, clear image; one that felt really at home inside the interior mileu which was continuing to form itself in her life.

The Energy Cloud, which is the Source of Nothing as well as Everything, and The MORE also, seemed to not make sense to Expander. "But" she said, "it is really the Life-Energy that is totally clear on everything, that makes sense of everything and helps to put things in order for us humans." She was realizing that the real question is, From where are we viewing or listening to the Cloud?

Sort of sorting through stuff so far, Expander (kind of) heard this within herself: "humans are energy; energy has frequencies; at our higher potentials, humans are higher frequencies. Everything, in fact, is energy and therefore is on a certain frequency. If we are paying attention to the Cloud, (of which we are an un-detachable part) from a different frequency than the one which the Cloud is on, we are getting partial signal.

It's much like listening to a radio station that is only partially tuned in to the exact station and therefore we only hear certain amounts of what is coming back to our speakers, yet it is distinguishable enough to actually grasp some key modules of the transmission.

Tuning in more often to the Energy, for longer periods of time is a practice Expander likes doing and wants to do. "I may not be completely on the exact frequency of the Energy Cloud, but I am definitely getting in on its frequency, that much is unmistakable", she said almost out loud. Realizing that the Energy makes sure to be affirming and confirming of that which is being transmitted, mostly by how it feels like actual LIFE and Understanding. The fact that it is totally Unconditional is mesmerizing.

Feeling rather like she was in a "zone", Expander wandered into her day feeling complete inner-calm, had a tranquil smile on her face which seemed to match the state of her interior organs, and felt as if her steps were so light she may have been gliding. That was her unbreakable Oneness connection with source letting her know she was "on".

Expander met her friend Shifter in the park for a smoothie and a walk, then went through her day enjoying herself along the way, whatever she was doing, wherever she went, whomever she met, until…. Expander encountered Logistical.

Logistical is from The Little Box era of Expander's life. Being an energy frequency, Expander briefly wondered how she attracted the energy of "The Little Box" into her experience today. "Well, All is One, One is All. I welcome everyone and everything, appreciating the role everything and everyone plays in my life and unveiling of The MORE. I trust the Comprehensively Wise Higher Mind of the Energy Cloud", she said to herself.

As they spoke while briefly passing on their respective paths, Logistical was openly curious about Expander's adventures and "living so far outside the box", stating that she really should be reasonable about what she does, the risks she takes and the things she intends to do. The genuine smile on Expander's face, rooted deeply in her Core Energetic Being was really the answer to Logistical's concerns and response to his advice, but Expander answered verbally as well- "Everything keeps working out and I'm enjoying my life every day, thank you for asking. Enjoy your day today as well, Logistical!" she said pivoting to continue enjoying her life today as well.

It wasn't that Expander thought Logistical is a "bad" person, she just knew they now had different paths, choices, and perspectives in regards to the world. Logistical being more convinced that there was only a "material" world with no unseen energetic resources within, she did not try to convince him to see her newly discovered energy-based understanding of "reality". She did acknowledge to herself that her energy vibration was always emanating out from herself (just like everyone's is) only now hers had far more clarity, love and life-givingness in it since she had been leaning into the Energy Cloud more readily.

Leaning into the Energy Cloud, of which we are each a "section", gradually reveals that it's actually impossible to lean into it. Expander found herself here again. She pondered "What is in process is the progressive realization that we are the "Cloud", we are the Energy. It is so much bigger than us, eh, uh, so much bigger that it can't be measured because everyone, everything is also, All That Is. Weird!"

"Yes", she said to herself. "This new understanding does seem weird alongside the way things were modeled and assumed and taught earlier in life, but life actually works now." So, Expander's thought patterns were opening up, continuing to expand and the practiced neuron connections were disconnecting in order to re-connect in a different configuration.

Tuning into the Cloud (which protruded into her being) was actually changing her life to something that works.

How does tuning into this Energy Cloud shift a person to a life that actually works? Shifter asked Expander a few hours later when Expander was telling him about her experiences and learnings. Shifter had also gotten out of a box and met Expander with the others out in the Nothingness where Everything was. Though he was actually living more attuned to the Energy Cloud of which he is a portion, he was not well-versed in the data of what was happening or how to explain it.

Expander responded a little differently than Shifter anticipated, "it may not actually matter that you don't see or understand how it works, just that you experience it working, at least for now", she briefed Shifter. Shifter is one of those people who just makes the shift as he senses it is time.

Shifter seems to rock along in life experiencing experiences. He's become aware of himself and how different things seem to unroll for him the easiest, the funnest way that seemed natural to himself. He replied to Expander "I think I know what you mean. Whenever I watch other humans appear to think they are "lost" on what to do next because they are not so aware of who they are, not very attentive to their inner voice....I can see in those moments, that I am that.

"I Am That". Shifter felt a glimpse of what he was saying when he spoke those words. Shifter was beginning to get a felt-clue about being One with the Energy Cloud of which all else and everyone else is also a section. To say "I am that" is at least a degree or beginning of recognition of the oneness of All that Is. "This Energy Cloud thing is something of an enigma, but ever so fascinating", said Shifter to Expander. "I'm experiencing some sense about it within myself.

I can tell something is feeling different- it's a good feeling-different. Somehow it all makes comprehensive sense by how it feels....or something like that". Transitioning from years of trying to understand through physical eyes and ears to sensing it through the Energy's vibration takes some adjustment.

Expander explained to Shifter what she has been learning about gaining perspective through non-physical eye and ears- "It's like using a different interior muscle you never knew you had, IF you didn't know you had used it before", she said. "Many people swear by listening to your 'inner voice' or your 'intuition', or your 'gut". That is simply the Energy Cloud with which we are all One, nudging the person in their preferred direction through energetic vibration". Expander continued, "It may or may not be necessary to know these details, the underneath understanding of what is going on, but some humans enjoy it, want it, or need it in order to make the shifts they desire to make for themselves".

"Leaning into the Energy Cloud just feels good", Shifter told Expander. "I know I have long been experiencing a sense of this reality in my own core being. At times, I've referred to it as my 'soul'". In any case, I will continue to do what feels good to me inside, like I always have. Only now that I have attracted in more understanding, I can be more intentional about my interactions with the Cloud".

Expander and Shifter chatted a little further, happy that they can share their experiences "listening to" or, "feeling for" the vibrations of the Life Giving Energy of which they are both expressions in a human body. Knowing a little more about Core Reality, puts some sense of order or arrangement of how things work For we humans, in the world, as we further Tune In to Who and What we Are: The Energy Cloud

Written by John-Randall J.R. Hofheins 2017

Expander's New Nexts

The New Frequency Fable series, v4

John-Randall "J.R." Hofheins

2017

Expanding ever, at some points obvious, at others not even detected until afterward, Expander is having fun playing in the Energy of the Energy Cloud as if a child in a sandbox. Only in this scenario, the energy behaves more like clay than sand.

Expander, coming to see that she wanted to change some things in her life, leaned closer in to the ever- flowing energy. This again, in order to get a better sense for what is actually going on in non-physical so she could feel out what she wants to do from here in the physical. She began to get a totally different angle on things-next.

"I'm wondering" said Expander, "how do new things come about for me? The way new opportunities and options have seemed to come to many around me most of my life has appeared to be luck or happenstance. Often it took physically managing life, relational connections and work intersections in order to get the next thing that person wanted. But that's not looking or feeling the same now while I get a new sense from the Energy Cloud". Expander was uncovering something she had not understood before.

What she was discovering, was that since we are Creators, we are the initiators-"Oh, I SEE!" said Expander. We don't go looking for New Next things, we create them". It was there that the peep hole through which Expander was peering into the next thing, that the peep hole became a porthole and was turning into a window. She was grasping the process now that she understood the fact that she herself was the prime initiator of everything she experiences.

The ethereal further-opening port-hole found an easiness-to-believe within Expander about what she wanted next. In general, she wants an enjoyable life scenario which includes the basic components of fun, easy-going loving relationships, enjoyable creative opportunities through which she gets paid, comfortable housing and fitting-for-her transportation. THAT was the feel she had for her next, in broader generalities.

Expander could feel into this scenario at this point and acknowledge that "all of this feels good to me. Each component and the entire picture as well." She immediately smiled knowingly since she could tell internally that her Core Being, her Higher Self agreed with all of this. She, so far, had no disagreeing thought patterns to compete with her new desired next.

Feeling this good about the process of unveiling what is next for her, Expander thought herself into…"more detail feels called for at this point. After enjoying my current role at YtechtL, I'm feeling like I may want to do some similar things on my own". She began to feel the "sun go down" within her a bit. It was like the rays of light being obscured. Expander did not feel as good as she had been feeling. It was clear that her Inner/Higher Self was feeling something different about the more detailed idea.

Expander returned to the bigger picture idea with all the general components in it, felt good again, then went on her way carrying that feeling with her.

It felt good all day; every time she re-visited the interior scenario it was lit up brightly. She felt the fun of the way life was working for her, even in the process. She knew that seeing the life-set-up inside her while feeling the enjoyment of it, was indication that it was already materializing in her life. The enjoyable feeling of it was what she was feeling for anyway.

The enjoyable feeling within. "Hmmm, Expander pondered. That is really what I want. It's what I always want- The Enjoyable Feeling of the something new. After the something new comes, I enjoy it expressing in my physical life for a while until it feels like I've exhausted it's fun rather soon after its appearing. I want to ponder this more", she said.

After leaning into the Cloud (in the name of "pondering"), Expander realized that this is the way life is, "We are all expanding, shifting further, allowing new experiences into our lives. Even though we've been taught to be "satisfied with what you have", that's not the actuality of the universe. The universe and all that is in it is expanding, getting better, more refined. Therefore it is congruent and makes feeling-sense that I am expanding into new nexts all along the way as well. It is usual, normal, aligned with Core Source Reality for me to want more, More and MORE".

Expander was releasing the idea that it was selfish or greedy to want more, More, MORE, as she also let in the actuality of how things are with the Universe. "It is all arranged very nicely to fit well at every shift and move. As I keep staying attuned to the Energy Cloud, which is actually my Higher Self, Higher Mind, I can't go wrong. In fact, things are set up so that even if I am not tuning in to my SELF, I feel the contrasting feelings that prompt me to go tune-in, lean in to Source of Life Energy Cloud again. That experience indicates I keep expanding, which leads to more new desires!"- She felt a crescendo of excitement that clarified the way for her to really be her true, authentic self.

With new levels of enthusiasm, Expander continued to focus on, feel around the general life-scenario that felt good to her in that form. She then began sifting through to see which details might want to come through further, "I could tell which, by how each felt to me", she noted.

Expander went on sifting through the images and ideas coming to her imagination, removing old unuseful thought patterns that mitigated against what she felt like she wanted. She was discovering the realization, the materialization of what began as a desire within her. She said "the peep-hole became a port-hole… became a widening window until it became a door through which I could take natural physical steps". Aware that she felt like a very different being than she did when she began with an oblique desire, a tiny opening to the New Next with increasing energy had increased to the progressive unveiling. Unveiling?

"Unveiling", Expander discerned, seemed to her like a much more accurate term to describe what is going on. "I am the one who is changing, not the physical realm", she acknowledged. "Everything being energy, I tune my own frequency to what I want to experience and it gradually happens at whatever rate my belief system will allow with clarity. The more clear my belief system is, the quicker I realize what I want."

She was aware that if her thought patterns have set up something of a "belief" complex-enough or seemingly "fixed" that it would be more of a process. She was aware that she might either want to move on to something else to create, or to allow whatever approximation of her current desire, to partially come in now. "I could see the approximation as a simple next step in the progressive unveiling of the ultimate thing I think I want. It also may be that after living the alternative version, I may then want something totally different. Everything is always moldable, more like clay than sand", Expander explained to her earth-mind self.

"Even though, I am playing life in a sand box, the energy is my modeling clay. I can always reshape whatever I am making. Life in the physical is a continual creation event that has no ending point. I can keep having fun by forming the situations I then get paid to solve resulting others feel relief. I construct scenarios where I make people laugh and feel the flow of the Life Force Energy Cloud. It's even possible for me to open to the Life-Giving Energy Cloud for simple ideas on inventions that make life easier for humans all across the planet. The possibilities never end. Whatever is enjoyable to me is beneficial to others as well, whether it's millions or one. I love all of my New Nexts!"

So, Expander scooted off to feel out which Next New Nexts were ready for her to bring them into being in the physical. Will it be physical, visible substance or something fun to experience by herself and others. Who knows, she may do both.

Expander in this fable, is demonstrating that we seem to be THE initiators of what we experience. At some point we have to realize who we actually are and of what we are capable. This necessitates that each give up the victim approach to life, possess who we ARE on higher and lower registers, collaborate with our higher-minded-Self, with deference. That basically is the key to moving forward (and upward in frequency).

The old way of waiting for some unknown someone to do something to take care of you, blaming someone who did something to you, protesting the government officials, getting angry with the "machine" (wherever it may be found), depending upon someone else to come be the trigger puller for taking a step....is over. This is a new era. We are no longer company bitches, in whatever small way that construct may still be installed. It is sneaky when it is small and hunkered down in a corner of us.

This new era calls for each of us to give up un-useful thought-patterns, ideas, approaches to life and live by our own higher thought patterns. We can live lives more freely and spaciously; lives that work albeit from a different basis than we thought. This new era calls for higher frequency living in realized connection with the Energy Cloud that is us. That Life-Energy is the seedbed from which all things sprout and grow.

Live life on your own terms the way that feels best to you. Consider if this little fable or anything else I've written, helps you get clear on who you are, what you want and what you are able to do beyond what you have experienced thus far....or not.

Higher frequency living as Higher Frequency Humans is about being your own "government" and allowing everyone else to be theirs. That is Love.

From my Universe to Yours,

John-Randall "J.R." Hofheins

2017

Other Opuscule publications by J.R. Hofheins

New Frequency Fables

Expander and the Little Box, v1

Expander and the MORE v2

Expander and the Energy Cloud v3

Expander's New Nexts v4

Expander uncovers NOW v5

Higher Frequency Perspectives series

Humans are Higher Frequencies: Who humans are and of what we are capable

Higher Frequency Therapy: Unveiling Higher Identities and Infinite Capacities

Higher Frequency Parenting: Freely and Lightly

LifeGiving Divorce Perspectives: Remaining in Your Identity Through Processes of Change

"Things are almost never as they first appeared, nor at second through 10th glance, keep humbly attending with openness- IF you want to KNOW"

"We were all (generally) taught to live backwards. If we begin with any basic premise other than that the world is energy, we end up haphazardly building worlds in which we silently act as if something external has control over us, making us dependent bitches, victims".

by John Randall Hofheins November 2017

Expander Uncovers NOW

New Frequency Fables v5

John-Randall "J.R." Hofheins

2017

Time after time, Expander got glimpses of the fact...

……………………………….that there isn't any.

Looking back, she could see, sense, even feel the same feelings now that she did then. Of course the next day, she could do it again. So, future, past, present seems to Expander to all be NOW.

Paying attention to fractions of our earth experience in bite-sized segments, Expander found that she can attend to life while attuned to the Energy Cloud more easily- "and it is more fun that way", she said.

At any point of check-in, the day is always NOW. At every look at one of those devices with numbers on it from 1 to 12, it is always NOW. Yes, it is a challenge to "do away" with the idea of time altogether, but Expander found that "as I loosened up my terminology and thinking around the concept, I paid less attention to the devices like clocks, watches and calendars. The less attention I gave those devices, the more life broadened out and became more simple for me".

"Yes", she said, "it creates a very interesting interface with Logistical and others who were still preferring the practice of holding the concept of highly refined organization in place for themselves so sturdily, but I am liking living life more freely and lightly, more spaciously as less of that time-belief is in place.

We will gradually see what things look like over the energetic Earth experience we are having!" Expander said, "At this point I know it is NOW!"

Calendars always say NOW; Time is an illusion perspective, even while we have agreed- at least tacitly- that the clock tells us what hour, minute as well as which 60th of a minute it is NOW. Expander sat in the atmosphere of this idea she had been agreeing to for the extent of her life to-date, then discerned- "I really actually feel my body as more relaxed, and myself as more in-joy as I let some distance come between me and the idea of time. Going about my life bypassing the orienting of myself to clocks to determine what I "should" do next, feels so good. It is so good to feel like who I am...free and untethered to limits".

Expander continued for a while longer noticing all the ways she had allowed the illusion of "time" to control her life.

Time, clocks, calendars. What day of the week is it?. Which month does the training begin? How much time do I have before we have to head out? How old are you? Complete this form including your birthdate. "There seems to be something of a controlling-feel or at least a sense of grasping for a degree of control, in the timing ideas around days and nights", thought Expander.

"Hmmm. I wonder, how is life lived more surrendered to the free-flowing Energy Cloud of which I am actually an expression?", Expander had never entered this thought realm before. "How does this work?"

Time….Clocks…. watches. Sundials, earlier on. Day…and Night."….not sure about details yet, but I know I feel so much lighter and freer choosing to subject myself directly to my Source- the Energy Cloud- than to the confines of tightly formatted machines and ideas to which most humans choose to subject themselves. I'm going to explore this more", she said. "There seems to be lots of breadth, in fact infinite breadth and space around the Energy Cloud…hmmm….which is really who and what I actually AM…hmmm".

Lots of hmmmm'ing going on for Expander. The nature of what she felt from the essence of Energy Cloud is so real, so....well "it feels more like actual authentic life than anything associated with time and space....especially contrasted to trying to put things into tiny little segments like minutes and seconds", she half-wondered out loud, believingly.

"The obvious different sensation between living in time and space without thinking of the Energy Cloud then leaning into the Energy Cloud almost unable to think of time and space, is like night and day in fun quality" Expander noted to herself.

"The Energy Cloud clearly has it ALL, at least all that I need or want".

Expander wrote in her journal about her experiential exploration with energy that, "there seems to always be a level of contrivance, of artificiality when I pay attention purely to what I see around me for very long. It's okay for a while, then it pales in excitement. Whenever I slow down and pay attention to the Energy Cloud, sort of become One with it, everything there and on earth becomes clear; it's like I have understanding and balance and inner calm-knowing while tuned in there". Expander expressed her grasp of things so-far, and somehow knew that there was far more to unfold from her tuning into the energy cloud in her solitude moments.

While melding as One with the Life Energy she knew that she was getting part of the picture of clarity for herself and that there was always more beyond where she left off. It sort of felt as if that is the way it would always be- That she could get more clarity than the previous "leaning in" and that she may also get less, but it didn't matter, "as long as I keep feeling good all along the way" she thought.

Leaning in around the idea of "time", about feeling like it is always simply "NOW", Expander heard within herself "that nothing else really mattered". Then that idea began to follow her through her days. Expander noticed "I'm just carrying within myself the sense that the only thing that matters is NOW. Simultaneously, it sort of puts me in a place of feeling 'between two worlds'; I will see if that sorts itself out as I pay attention to the Energy from within my conscious being".

Expander noticed that as she was living in, looking at the already unveiled physical surroundings then leaning into the Energy over and over as a practice it began to show her more about time and space- "I'm automatically allowing the living Energy of the Cloud's clarity to make sense of the plethora of people organizing their lives by clocks and calendars". I can live either way, it's my choice. But what feels most alive, most real is the Cloud Energy or maybe the energy of the cloud brought into the physical realm. When I focus my attention that way, I notice that I can function in freedom and lightness".

Spaciousness begins to replace confinement. Expander had this phrase come to mind when she stopped somewhere in the latter part of the day simply for relaxing, to eat a chocolate ice cream cone while feeling the smile deeply within herself. Spaciousness replaces self-confinement, came again. "Spaciousness really feels good; even while I seem to now 'visit' arenas where clock and calendar are counted as Queen, I can function sort of outside that realm within myself. The Energy Cloud being totally wise knows how to do that, my earth mind simply receives the guidance".

Now….NOW! " I am getting other pieces of this fun picture puzzle that is unfathomable from the material-only physical realm", Expander said. "NOW, allows me to be in tune with the Cloud and all that it has to offer for life and love and understanding while playing in the physical environment". That physical environment, as she discovered earlier, was simply a mixture of all that everyone had collectively created either purposely or haphazardly. In any case, being at least a little more in open spaciousness more often, Expander kept receiving more understanding……

Expander elucidated for herself further, "When I simply live in the NOW, bypassing the confinement in which I had placed myself and which humanity generally chooses, I am experiencing spaciousness, freedom, lightheartedness; that is the essence of the Energy Cloud; I am part of the Cloud so I AM THAT also, I Am".

The more Expander enjoyed being who she expansively is; the more she appreciated the freedom of NOW, the more she experienced expansiveness within herself, expanding energetically into more of who she is, actually. "This is life unspeakable for me" said Expander, "I'm happier and happier; things keep working out for me so enjoyably and almost effortlessly. It's as if I have unseen help when I appreciate the NOW".

Expander, expanding into more expansiveness of her infinite SELF; an expression of the Cloud of Energy…..”Seems counter-logical to what I once knew, and what many people still know, but it certainly feels better and better”, she said. “I feel like who I was meant to be and ever more so. Although I feel as if I live on and from a different basis, a different platform than I once did. This basis gives everything the sense that life is far more effective….I mean, life works for me so fluidly; it's easier and more fun as if that's the way life is supposed to be for all of us. Life is definitely discovered, NOW”.

"Living life in the NOW is what thriving seems to be made of; It really feels as if it is the only environment in which authenticity is actual, at least for me, Expander said to her friends who had gradually gathered around her. They had thought she was off her rocker when the first few heard her mumbling to herself earlier in this thought process. They soon caught up with the vibration of her energy, which conveyed understanding for their earth minds to connect with Higher Frequency Mind. Tuning in always brings clarity and understanding which results in calmness within. Some of the realization comments from Expanders friends went something like this:

"NOW is real; dividing NOW into segments is an illusion."

"NOW, contains natural alignment with oneself;

trying to control NOW creates artificiality"

"NOW, is LIFE;

allowing artificial constructs to form life is its suppression"

"NOW, Live LIFE, NOW"

So for you, maybe from time to time, you could recognize with Expander that there isn't any….

…in order to LIVE Life more NOW, ongoingly….

WHAT BOX?

A platform for students and readers to describe their experience of moving to actual spacious living

After reading- *Further Outside the Box/ New Frequency Fables*

I absolutely enjoyed reading New Frequency Fables! It's a great read for someone who feels trapped in everyday life, who wants to lose a sense of time or who wants to live life more freely. This novel is not a step-by-step guide on what to do per se, but it will expand your mind on how to acquire personal fulfillment. No matter what aspect of life's journey you are currently on, I'm sure you'll find something that relates to your past, present or something you hope to experience in your future.

Chaz Randall

The box

At some point after the marriage, I began to knock down doors and walls about what I believed about relating in Love. At first this was scary. I had to imagine a world in which there was no love relationship, no marriage, no growing old together, no mutual aid it seemed. However, as I wandered further out from those ideas turning to see how confining and small it was, suddenly there was adventure in the wide open space outside those ideas.. Years later, it still feels that way and that teeny little box that was the old way is composting into dust as I tromp across Everest in search of ever new understanding and ideas.

You see, from this new ever fresh perspective, there is no way to relate in Love. It is constantly forming, reforming, falling apart and recreating itself. It has always been that way. It is only the human condition that wants to confine it with ideas of how it is SUPPOSED to be done. Truly each Love experience is like a snowflake, always beautiful and unique to itself (even when it stinks, because for some reason, those situations have the most learning and personal evolutionary leaps within them).

At the present ever changing perspective, I have learned that in this experience, we shall call Swaranjoti's, that perhaps the whole notion of having a single relationship that lasts till death seems positively absurd to me. Could it happen? Yes, because I am open to experiencing it all as it evolves which means there aren't expectations of old ideas. However, at nearly 50 years, I have learned how to truly enjoy and rely on myself. Those I decide to Love relate with, are usually at the same place of human learning I find myself and so we coincide as we learn, until we don't. Coming together to Love, when we are no longer aligned with what we believe or are learning for the sake of something called a relationship, seems limiting to both parties. Shouldn't we rather Love one another enough to release each other to the wind for more learning, evolving, adventuring? Could it be that is how Love works? Perhaps, and perhaps as I am learning that...I will get a new perspective that changes it all. How fantastically elegant and organic. No longer boxed in I can allow newness, changes, fluidity and flow.

Since stepping way far out from the box, my experiences and ideas of Love and sexual relations (which do not necessarily have to go together) have expanded broadly. I have seen people of all genders (including those "transitioning") find and interact in Love. The notions of asexuality, pansexuality, have obscured any relative discomfort that may have been present for bisexuality or homosexuality (though relating sexualy doesn't always mean Love..). My Godfather's very religious daughter married and then found multiple other men she Loved. The marriage stands strong (where all sexual loving exchange takes place) and romantic Love with several others also exists with transparent agreements between all parties. How spectacular that Love can be so big, so enriching to so many. In my old ideas of Love I was boxing in a nebulae of unbelievable beauty. I was confining my own luminosity, learning and experience. Now I just fling my arms wide and invite new experiences. I exert my preferences and hold firm boundaries about my safety and what I want. I invite only high level experiences with great communication and conscious focus on Loving in the highest way possible and unbelievable beauty has flowed through my life. Living the polyamorous Love relating I just described wouldn't work for me. I would be too scattered, but it works for them and I Love they get to experience so much beauty. When humans feel Love, beauty and acceptance the whole world changes for the better..

 I urge you, the reader, to sit within yourself peering deeply at your own beliefs of work, parenting, Loving, and helping/serving others and how those beliefs may be limiting your full authentic beautiful expression. Grab your fears by the horns, look them squarely in the eye. Tell them they are no longer necessary. Run headlong away from those boxes that APPEAR so safe and comfy and go out into the wide open spaces of your life. Live fully the white star dreams known in your ever expanding heart. The possibilities are endless. Your potential to BE whatever you want is just beyond the edge of the boxtop.

Swaranjoti Kaur

Further New Frequency Fables reading and further realizations/response to another Fable or segment of a fable that you might find helpful.I have to be honest, I thoroughly enjoyed New Frequency Fables. I enjoyed it more than the actual textbook. I had my reservations at first because I thought you just wanted us to buy a book that you personally wrote and that it was going to be a waste of my time. I don't really want to write much about our textbook, Sensations and Perceptions because it was boring. I also don't feel the need to lie about how the videos made me come to this big realization. I really want to expand on New Frequency Fables and how Expander Uncovers Now resonated with me. It discussed the concept of time and how it is an illusion perspective. What I took from this fable was that everyone has a birthdate and an expiration date, but what you decide to do with the time in between that period is completely up to you. A student

In the book New Frequency Fables in Volume 2 you stated "That was a part of how living works, was to feel a desire for something more; allow oneself to be okay with that something-unseen to come closer/ or take the inspired steps toward it; lean into the nothingness feeling expectantly; then it leads right back into one's ever expanding Self within. This statement could not be truer for myself. I have a burning desire for something more with my life.   A Student

[More entries to come]

J.R. Hofheins has been facilitating undergrad students to find their SELF-Clarity for several decades. He has been doing this from the "platform" of various Higher Ed posts as well as therapist roles, coordinator/director positions in non-profit youth-helping organizations and more. He lives in the serene environment of North Carolina mountains from where he teaches online, paints houses, serves beer to enjoyable customers and collaborates with students on various projects. His children and grand-children emit their clear-love signals into the world from various other states.   October 24, 2017

Gary Kociskewski is a graduate of Troy University in Troy, Alabama. He gets the energetic essence of the universe and is avidly practicing living his life deferring to that Life Energy. Gary is on a trajectory to teach at the university level at some point.

Chaz Randall is a first time mom, a student graduating from Troy University who is also grasping the nature of how tuning in to Life Energy connects the aspects of life so that things simply work for you. She is very adept at shifting her focus to whatever is life-giving for herself and her new born child. She is already impacting the world through her attention and intention for herself and her growing family.

Swaranjoti Kaur is a thoroughly deepening Kundalini Yoga Instructor. Her daily practice has unveiled for her, more of her true core SELF. She emanates the Life Energy of the Energy Cloud to her son, her therapy clients, her yoga students as well as to whomever her enlarging heart space points.

Section Finder for Further Outside the Box/New Frequency Fables

Expander and the New Nexts

Expander and the NOW

WHAT BOX?- Students and readers describe their shift to more spacious living

A bit about J.R. Hofheins

50411011R00078

Made in the USA
Columbia, SC
06 February 2019